Text © 2021 by Jane Kurtz
Illustrations © 2021 by John Joseph

Edited by Michelle McCann

Library of Congress Cataloging-in-Publication Data

Names: Kurtz, Jane, author. I Joseph, John, 1985- illustrator.
Title: Chickens on the loose / by Jane Kurtz ; illustrated by John Joseph.
Description: [Berkeley] : West Margin Press, [2021] · Audience: Ages 5-8. · Audience: Grades K-1. · Summary: Illustrations and easy-to-read, rhyming text follow a flock of chickens that gets loose and runs rampant through a city, causing mischief and mayhem. Includes information about keeping chickens in an urban environment.
Identifiers: LCCN 2020046905 (print) · LCCN 2020046906 (ebook)
    ISBN 9781513267241 (hardback) · ISBN 9781513267258 (ebook)
Subjects: CYAC: Stories in rhyme. · Chickens--Fiction. · City and town life--Fiction. · Humorous stories.
Classification: LCC PZ8.3.K957 Chi 2021 (print) · LCC PZ8.3.K957 (ebook) · DDC [E]--dc23
LC record available at https://lccn.loc.gov/2020046905
LC ebook record available at https://lccn.loc.gov/2020046906

Proudly distributed by Ingram Publisher Services

Printed in China
25 24 23 22 21 1 2 3 4 5

Published by West Margin Press

WEST MARGIN PRESS

WestMarginPress.com

WEST MARGIN PRESS
Publishing Director: Jennifer Newens
Marketing Manager: Angela Zbornik
Project Specialist: Micaela Clark
Editor: Olivia Ngai
Design & Production: Rachel Lopez Metzger

CHICKENS
ON THE LOOSE

By Jane Kurtz   Illustrated by John Joseph

WEST
MARGIN
PRESS

For my Portland neighbors (including sisters)—thanks for the eggs, the compost, the soothing sounds, and the stories of escaped chickens. —J.K.

For Jacob—thank you for the discerning eye. —J.J.

Chickens breaking loose.
Chickens on the lam.
Zipping from the yard,
as quickly as they can.

"Stop!" calls the girl. But the chickens will not stop.

Chickens on the loose, racing down the street.
Hopping up to window shop, clinging with their feet.

"Stop!"
yells the owner.

But the chickens
will not stop.

Chickens on the loose.
They trot. They lope. They jog.
They duck into a studio
to do some downward dog.

"Stop!" calls the yogi.
But the chickens will not stop.

Chickens getting hungry, peckish from the chase.

Taking stock, around the block
a lovely foodcart space!

"STOP!" shouts a cook.
But the chickens will not stop.

Chickens quick and nimble...

...run along the street,
hitch a ride on skateboards
to rest their aching feet.

Chickens spot some paint cans—red and green and blue.
They hop right off and quickly add an element or two.

"STOP!" calls a cop.
But the chickens will not stop.

No one can stop these chickens!
There's a city to explore.

They spot a hamster on a wheel.
They sneak into the store.

They tiptoe up and down the aisles and then slip out the door.

"STOP!" shouts everybody.
But the chickens will not stop.

"No way!" they say
"We will not stay."
It sounds like

BOC BOC BOC

Chickens dodge and scurry.
They have to get away!
Chickens in a hurry
They want more time to play.

Look out! Four dogs! A cat!
Chickens leap and hurdle.

The humans follow...

Chickens weary now.
Much too tired to squawk.

Much too tired to plot or plan.
Almost too tired to walk.

Chickens droop and yawn.
They flop down on a lawn.

Plop... Plop.

Rain drops.
They know they must go on.

Chickens safe at home,
soothing tired legs.
Time to put their feet up.
Maybe lay some eggs.

Chickens fat and happy,
snoozing on the roost.

Oops! Yikes!
That old mood strikes...

Chickens on the loose!

KEEPING URBAN CHICKENS

Many city dwellers love to keep chickens. Hens that are free to roam a yard eating bugs and grass lay eggs with great flavor. Here are some things to know:

- You will probably need to get a permit from your city. Most cities allow you to keep 4 to 6 chickens per yard and don't allow you to keep roosters. (Roosters can wake up neighbors WAY early.)

- Chickens need plenty of space in their coops and an outside area for exercise.

- If your hens are healthy and getting enough light (around 14 hours a day), they will usually lay 1 egg per day.

- Check to see if your city has a feed store. It's a good place to get chicks and information.

- You can also buy feed mixtures for your chickens at the feed store. Table scraps should only be snacks. Keep food and fresh water out constantly for chickens.

- Always wash your hands after handling chickens AND eggs.

- Chickens aren't great flyers, but they do like to explore. Check your fences regularly for holes. Chickens are curious and can squeeze through small openings. If one chicken tries something (like escaping), others usually follow.

- To learn more, check out *A Kid's Guide to Keeping Chickens* by Melissa Caughey.

MORE CHICKEN FACTS:

- Chickens don't like hanging out alone. They are social birds.

- Chickens are very vocal and will have clucky conversations with you.

- An egg develops for about 24 hours within a hen's body. The egg's color and pattern happen in the last few hours before it is laid.